SUGAR

SPICE . . .

AND EVERYTHING NICE . . .

These were the ingredients chosen to

create the perfect little girl.

But Professor Utonium accidentally

added an extra ingredient to

the concoction —

CHEMICAL X!

And thus, The Powerpuff Girls were born!

Using their ultra superpowers,

BLOSSOM,

BUBBLES,

and **BUTTERCUP**

have dedicated their lives to fighting crime

and the forces of evil!

FRIGHTY NIGHT

CARTOON NETWORK®

by E. S. Mooney
Based on
"THE POWERPUFF GIRLS,"
as created by Craig McCracken

SCHOLASTIC INC.

New York Toronto London Auckland Sydney
Mexico City New Delhi Hong Kong Buenos Aires

No part of this publication may be reproduced in whole or in part, or stored in a retrieval system, or transmitted in any form or by any means, electronic, mechanical, photocopying, recording, or otherwise, without written permission of the publisher. For information regarding permission, write to Scholastic Inc., Attention: Permissions Department, 555 Broadway, New York, NY 10012.

ISBN 0-439-29591-2

Copyright © 2001 by Cartoon Network.
CARTOON NETWORK, the logo, THE POWERPUFF GIRLS and all related characters and elements are trademarks of and © Cartoon Network.
(s01)

Published by Scholastic Inc. All rights reserved.
SCHOLASTIC and associated logos are trademarks and/or registered trademarks of Scholastic Inc.

Designed by Peter Koblish
Illustrated by Ken Edwards

12 11 10 9 8 7 6 5 4 3   2 3 4 5 6/0

Printed in the U.S.A.
First Scholastic printing, October 2001

The city of Townsville, home of The Power-puff Girls, the cutest little superheroes in the world! It's another happy day at Pokey Oaks Kindergarten. It's an especially happy day! An especially special happy day! An especially special super — okay, you get the idea.

Ms. Keane, the teacher, stood in front of the classroom. Behind her was a brightly colored calendar.

"All right, class," Ms. Keane said cheerfully. "Who can tell me what the weather is like today?"

Bubbles volunteered. "Today is a pretty day with lots of sunshine!" she said.

"Very good, Bubbles," Ms. Keane replied. "Let's use our Mr. Sun sticker." She picked a sticker with a big smiling sun from the side of the calendar.

Blossom's arm shot into the air. "Oh, Ms. Keane!"

"Yes, Blossom?" Ms. Keane replied.

"It's actually only *mostly* sunny right now," Blossom reported. "There is a five percent cumulus cloud cover."

"Oh — well, thank you, Blossom," Ms. Keane said. "I'm afraid we don't have a sticker that shows that, though. So we'll just stick with Mr. Sun."

Buttercup crossed her eyes and stuck

her tongue out at her sister. "Show-off," she grumbled.

Ms. Keane turned to the class. "Now, who knows what day it is today?"

"I know! I know!" came the chorus of replies from the class. The students were all waving their hands in the air. Some were even jumping up and down. Harry Pit was groaning as if he were about to burst.

"My goodness, how enthusiastic everyone is today," Ms. Keane said with a smile. "Yes, Harry, why don't you tell us what day it is."

A huge grin spread across Harry's face. "Today's the opening day for Dinkley's Amusement Park!" he announced.

The other children began to cheer.

Ms. Keane smiled. "Children, I know you're all excited about the new amusement park —"

"You bet!" Buttercup yelled.

"Dinkley's is the biggest amusement park ever built in Townsville," Blossom added.

"And the funnest!" Bubbles cried.

"I'm going tomorrow!" Mitch Mitchelson announced.

"I'm going right after school," Harry declared.

"Children, I have to admit even *I* am excited about the amusement park," Ms. Keane told them. "I have plans to go this weekend, too. But right now we need to settle down and get back to work. Now, who can tell me what day it is?"

Poor kids. It's so hard to sit still and learn —

especially when the biggest amusement park in Townsville history is about to open!

Later that afternoon! Our three happy little superheroes are heading home from school.

As Blossom, Bubbles, and Buttercup flew along, they could see crowds of people below them. Everyone was hurrying in the direction of the amusement park.

"It looks like practically everyone in

Townsville is going to the new amusement park," Blossom commented.

"Maybe the Professor will let us go," Bubbles said.

"Let's tell him about it as soon as we get home," Buttercup decided.

They flew by a crumbling brick wall with some old trash cans in front of it.

"Look!" Buttercup said. "The Gangreen Gang aren't on their usual corner!"

The Gangreen Gang were five no-good-niks — Ace, Big Billy, Snake, Grubber, and Little Arturo. The gang was known for writing graffiti, making crank phone calls, and bullying schoolchildren.

"Maybe they went to the amusement park," Buttercup said.

Bubbles giggled. "I guess bad guys like to have fun, too!"

The Girls continued on their way home. They zoomed through the front door of their house and into the kitchen. Professor Utonium was waiting for them.

"Why, hello, Girls," the Professor said. "I hope you had a good day at school. I've prepared a nice, wholesome snack for you."

The Girls began to buzz around the Professor's head like a swarm of bees.

"Professor, the new amusement park is opening today!" Blossom said.

"Can we go?" Buttercup demanded.

"Pretty please, with sugar on top?" Bubbles pleaded. "And syrup and sprinkles and a cherry?"

The Professor chuckled. "I read all about the amusement park in the newspaper, Girls. Of course you can go."

"Yay!" Bubbles sang out.

"Hooray!" Blossom cried.

"All right!" Buttercup yelled.

"But not on a school night," the Professor said. "You know the rules. No outside activities on school nights — except for fighting monsters and bad guys, that is."

The three Girls' faces fell.

"You can go first thing on Saturday," the Professor finished. "Now, how about starting on that wholesome snack I made you?"

Poor Powerpuff Girls. Saturday is two whole days away! But even superheroes have to follow the rules.

The next day at Pokey Oaks. Uh-oh, what's this? Why does everyone look so glum? What happened to all those joyful, smiling faces from yesterday? What's going on here?

Bubbles sat in the Drawing Area with Mary Thompson, Elmer Sglue, and Wes Goingon. Bubbles loved the Drawing Area. She loved to make pretty pictures of pretty rainbows and flowers.

"Did you hear what happened to Harry

Pit when he went to the amusement park yesterday?" Mary asked.

"I bet he had tons and tons and tons of fun," Bubbles said. She reached for a pink crayon to start drawing a pretty flower.

"Yeah, if you call being captured by a zombie fun!" Mary said.

Bubbles froze. A zombie! That sounded scary.

"That's not true, Mary," Wes said.

Bubbles breathed a sigh of relief. "Phew, that's good! 'Cause if Harry was captured by a zombie that would be really, really, really —"

Wes cut her off. "It wasn't a zombie, it was a Frankenstein monster! And it didn't capture him, it ate him!"

Bubbles's blue eyes widened. "What kind of amusement park has zombies and Frankenstein monsters?" She was a little worried. She and her sisters were supposed to go to Dinkley's tomorrow.

"A haunted one," Wes said. "And Dinkley's Amusement Park is definitely haunted!"

Bubbles gulped. *Could it be true?*

Meanwhile, in the Block Building Area . . .
Buttercup was playing with Lloyd and Floyd Floijoidson. They were building a huge tower. As soon as it was done they planned to smash it.

"Hey, did you hear about the amuse-ment park?" Floyd asked.

"Don't tell me anything!" Buttercup commanded. "I want to be surprised when I go there tomorrow."

Floyd and Lloyd began to snicker.

"Okay, we won't tell you," Floyd said.

"If you're *sure* you don't want to know," Lloyd said.

"If you're *sure* you still want to go tomorrow," Floyd added.

"What is it?" Buttercup demanded.

"You said you didn't want us to tell you," Lloyd pointed out.

"You said you wanted to be surprised tomorrow," Floyd agreed.

Buttercup grabbed each boy by the neck. "Tell me right now — if you want to *live* till tomorrow!" she said.

The boys tried to talk, but their voices wouldn't come out. Buttercup released them.

"The amusement park is haunted," Lloyd said. "My cousin Daphne went yesterday, and she says it's full of ghosts and goblins and zombies and monsters."

"So what?" Buttercup said. "I ain't afraid of no ghosts!"

"What about goblins and zombies and monsters?" Floyd asked.

"Not them, either," Buttercup said. She struck a fighting pose. "Bring 'em on!"

Meanwhile, in the Rocket Science/Space and Aeronautic Design Area . . .

Blossom was the only one sitting in the Rocket Science/Space and Aeronautic Design Area. She was always the only one in the Rocket Science/Space and Aeronautic Design Area. In fact, it was Blossom who had convinced Ms. Keane to *have* a Rocket Science/Space and Aeronautic Design Area.

Blossom was busy drawing a scale model of a rocket ship. But she was also listening to the other conversations in the room — to what the other kids were saying about the amusement park. And she thought the whole thing was ridiculous. Blossom knew there was no such thing as a haunted amusement park.

After a few minutes, Mitch Mitchelson came over to where Blossom was working.

"Did you hear about the amusement park?" he asked.

"*What* about the amusement park?" Blossom said impatiently.

"You know," Mitch said, "that it's haunted. You know what happened to

Harry there, don't you?" Mitch made a slicing motion across his neck. Then he fell backward as if he were dead.

"That's the trouble with Harry," Blossom said. "I mean the trouble with all these stories about Harry. Nobody knows the real truth, and everybody's just getting scared by all these silly rumors!"

She put down the model she was working on and went over to see Ms. Keane.

"Ms. Keane, I think it's time to call a classroom meeting," Blossom said. "A lot of the kids are spreading rumors about the amusement park and Harry, and everyone's getting really scared."

Ms. Keane didn't look like her usual cheerful self. She nodded. "That's a good idea, Blossom," she said.

Ms. Keane called all the children out to

the yard. "Children, I know that a lot of
you have been talking about what you
think might have happened to Harry Pit,"
she began.

*Okay, here it comes. Now Ms. Keane will
set everything straight. Harry probably just
ate too much cotton candy and has a stom-
achache today.*

"Nobody is quite sure what happened to
Harry," Ms. Keane went on.

"Huh?" Blossom said.

Huh?

"We know that he had a bad scare yesterday at the amusement park," Ms. Keane said. "Whatever it was, he can't even talk about it today. He's going to be all right, but he just needs to rest for a few days."

"Oh, poor Harry," Bubbles said, her lower lip quivering.

"My dad says I can't go to the amusement park at all — he says the place is haunted," Julie volunteered.

"Who'd want to go to a place like that?" Wes asked.

"Not me!" Floyd said.

"Me, either!" Lloyd added.

"I've canceled my plans to go this weekend as well," Ms. Keane admitted.

Blossom couldn't stand it anymore.

"This is ridiculous! There's no such thing as a haunted amusement park, and everyone knows it!"

"Tell that to the ghosts and zombies," Mitch said.

Buttercup stood up. "I've got something to tell those ghosts and zombies, all right!" she threatened.

"Me, too!" Blossom added, standing up beside her sister.

They turned to look at Bubbles.

"Me, too, I guess," Bubbles piped up nervously.

Ms. Keane didn't say anything. But the worried look hadn't left her eyes.

Chapter 3

Later that day! Our super little superheroes are on their way home from school once more. But the once-merry mood in Townsville has changed . . .

As Blossom, Bubbles, and Buttercup flew over Townsville, they could see crowds of people below them once again. But this time, the crowds were running in the opposite direction, *away* from the amusement park. They were trailing tickets for rides, popcorn, and cotton candy behind them.

"Boy, this rumor has really caught on," Blossom commented.

"H-how do we know for sure that it is a rumor?" Bubbles asked.

"Because there's no such thing as ghosts, zombies, goblins, mummies, or any of that stuff!" Blossom said.

"And if there were, we'd just beat 'em up!" Buttercup added.

"Somebody's got to prove to everyone that there's nothing to be afraid of," Blossom said. "That's why we're going to that amusement park tomorrow as planned!"

"Yeah!" Buttercup agreed. "We'll show everyone that The Powerpuff Girls aren't afraid of anything!"

Bubbles didn't say anything.

That's all right, Bubbles. We know you're afraid of some things — like sleeping without a night-light, and scary stories, and when you turn off the lamp and the chair in your room starts to look like a mean old witch.

The Girls continued on their way home. They zoomed through the front door of their house and into the kitchen.

"Why, hello, Girls," the Professor said. "I hope you had a good day at school. I've prepared a nice, wholesome snack for you. Oh, and I thought you might want to see this."

The Professor showed them the latest copy of the *Townsville Tribune*. Across the front of the paper in huge letters was the headline: NEW AMUSEMENT PARK — HAUNTED!

"Sorry, Girls, but you won't be able to go tomorrow after all," the Professor said.

"Haunted! Closed down!" Blossom cried.

"That's not fair!" Buttercup yelled.

"Oh, well, too bad. We'll just have to think of something else," Bubbles said quickly. "How about the zoo?"

Just then, the hotline rang. It was a special phone the Mayor of Townsville used to call the Girls whenever there was trouble. Blossom answered it. "Hello?"

The Mayor was on the other end of the line. "Oh, hi, Blossom, how nice to hear from you," he said.

"Mayor, *you're* the one who called *me*," Blossom reminded him. "What is it? Is Townsville in trouble?"

"Oh, yes, right," the Mayor said. "Well,

Blossom, it's about this new amusement park. Everyone's saying it's haunted, and I'd like you Girls to —"

Suddenly, the Mayor was cut off. Blossom could hear the sounds of a struggle in the background.

"Mayor, Mayor, what is it?" Blossom asked. "Are you all right?"

But the Mayor didn't answer.

Blossom hung up the phone and turned

to her sisters. "The Mayor's in trouble," she said. "He was calling to ask us to do something about the amusement park, and in the middle of it something happened. I think he's been kidnapped!"

"Oh, poor Mayor," Bubbles said, her eyes brimming with tears.

"Let's go find out who did it and beat 'em up!" Buttercup said.

"Right," Blossom agreed. "And I have a feeling I know just where to look. Come on, Girls, to the amusement park!"

"But it's closed," Bubbles objected.

"That's not gonna stop us!" Buttercup said.

"And it's a weeknight," Bubbles added.

"Bubbles, it's Friday. And while Friday is technically a weekday, which would make Friday night a weeknight, it's not a school night because we don't have school tomorrow, which is Saturday. Now come on!" Blossom said.

"Yeah, are you a Powerpuff Girl or a Punypuff Girl?" Buttercup challenged.

That was enough for Bubbles. "I'm a Powerpuff Girl!" she cried.

The Girls flew out the door. "Bye, Professor!" they called.

"Wait! Girls! What about your wholesome snack?" the Professor called after them. "Do you want me to pack it up in a brown bag for you?"

Too late, Professor. The Girls are off. The Mayor and the amusement-park-loving citizens of Townsville need them — now!

Chapter 4

When the Girls arrived at the amusement park, they found it dark and deserted. The big, lit-up sign that usually
said DINKLEY'S AMUSEMENT PARK was shut
off, and the entrance gate was closed.

"This is kind of spooky," Bubbles said.

"There's nothing at all to be afraid of,"
Blossom reassured her.

Just then, they heard a scream in the
distance.

"Wh-what was that?" Bubbles asked.

"A horrible, Bubbles-eating zombie!" Buttercup teased.

"Come on, Girls, let's go investigate," Blossom said, leading the way.

The three Girls flew in over the closed gate. All around them were deserted, motionless rides. They heard the scream again.

"Come on," Blossom said, zooming off again. "It came from this direction."

The Girls passed over the carousel and flew by the spinning teacups. Then they spotted one ride that was running. Several small cars ran at top speed along a track that spun in circles and turned upside down. A flashing sign above the ride said THE MYSTERY MACHINE.

The Mayor was strapped into one of the cars. He didn't seem to be enjoying his

ride. "He-e-e-elp!" he screamed. "Some-body get me out of here!"

Blossom zoomed over to the ride's control booth. She reached inside to pull the lever. The ride slowed to a halt.

Bubbles and Buttercup flew up to the top, where the Mayor's car was stranded.

"Don't worry, Mayor, we'll save you!" Bubbles said.

Tufts of white hair were sticking out

from the sides of the Mayor's head. His face looked a little green.

"Bubbles! Buttercup!" he cried when he saw the two Girls. "Thank goodness you're here! What a long ride! I'm glad it's over!"

Bubbles and Buttercup unstrapped the Mayor from his seat and floated back down to the ground with him. They put him down, and he wobbled dizzily. Blossom zoomed over to help him.

"Who did this to you?" Blossom asked.

"Oh, it was terrible!" the Mayor said. "There was a tall, white, sheety thing!"

"Sheety thing?" Buttercup asked. "You mean a ghost?"

"Yes, that's it," the Mayor said. "And there was another thing all wrapped in bandages, too."

"A mummy?" Bubbles asked.

"Yes, that's right," the Mayor said. "And then there was another thing with green skin and eyeballs that stuck out —"

"All right, that's enough!" Blossom cut him off. "There's no such thing as ghosts or mummies or any of this stuff!"

Just then there was a low moan from somewhere nearby.

"What do you call that?" Buttercup said.

They all turned to look. A mummy, wrapped from head to toe in bandages, had stepped out from behind a deserted ticket booth.

Everyone screamed.

"Yikes!" the Mayor cried, leaping into Blossom's arms. "Let's get out of here!"

chapter 5

"Wait a minute!" Buttercup said. "We're not afraid! We're The Powerpuff Girls!"

"Yeah!" Blossom said, putting the Mayor down. "Come on, Girls, let's get him!"

The mummy began to run away.

Go, Girls, go!

"Wait!" the Mayor cried. "You can't just leave me here!"

The Girls zoomed back. Blossom grabbed the Mayor, and they took off after the mummy again. But the mummy had disappeared behind a cotton candy stand. The Girls looked everywhere, but they couldn't find him.

Blossom put the mayor back down. "Mmmm, cotton candy," he said, reaching for some. "I'm definitely in the mood for a snack."

Suddenly, there was an eerie howl. A ghost popped out from behind a booth.

"Ooooooo!" the ghost said. "Ooooooo! Ooooooo!"

"Help!" the Mayor cried. He leaped into Buttercup's arms.

"Mayor!" Buttercup cried in disgust. She dropped him and took off after the ghost. "Let me at him! I'll tear him limb from limb!"

"He doesn't have any limbs," Blossom

pointed out, joining in the chase. "But let's get him anyway!"

"Don't forget me!" the Mayor cried.

With a sigh of frustration, Buttercup came back. She picked up the Mayor by the tails of his coat. The three Girls chased after the ghost.

But the Girls looked everywhere, and they couldn't find him.

Buttercup placed the Mayor back on the boardwalk. "Mmmm, ice cream," he said, reaching for a cone. "My favorite!"

Suddenly, there was a loud bellow, a horrible screech, and some evil laughter. A Frankenstein monster, a zombie, and a goblin appeared.

"Yow!" the Mayor yelled, jumping into Bubbles's arms.

"Oh, poor Mayor," Bubbles said. She rocked him a little to make him feel better.

The Frankenstein monster bellowed. He was huge and heavy. Bolts stuck out from the sides of his neck.

"Let's get 'em, Girls!" Blossom commanded.

The zombie screeched. He had green skin and horrible eyes that bugged straight out from their sockets. His tongue hung out of his mouth.

"Let's beat 'em up!" Buttercup yelled.

The goblin laughed an evil laugh. He was tiny.

"Aw, that one's kind of cute," Bubbles said.

Together, with the Mayor in tow, the

Girls took off after the Frankenstein monster, the zombie, and the goblin.

They flew past the fun house. They zoomed by the flumes. They whipped by the whip. But it was no use. The ghoulish villains kept splitting up and running off in different directions. They seemed to know the amusement park inside and out. Then the mummy and the ghost reappeared and joined in the mayhem. The Girls, dragging the Mayor behind them, just couldn't keep up.

Suddenly, Blossom yelled out, "Stop!"

Bubbles froze. Buttercup, who was carrying the Mayor piggyback, came to a halt.

"Look!" Blossom said. "The goblin just dropped something!"

She reached down and picked up a shiny object from the ground.

"It looks like a knife!" Buttercup said.

"Let's open it and see," Blossom said. She flipped the object open at its hinge. "It's not a knife, it's a comb!"

"A comb?" Bubbles looked bewildered. "Why would a goblin need a comb?"

"Good question!" Blossom said. She considered for a moment and then smiled. "Girls, it's time to set a trap!"

A trap? Blossom, what are you up to? Is that comb a clue of some kind?

chapter 6

"Okay, here's what we do," Blossom said, lowering her voice. "Those creepy creatures have been attacking people who come to use the amusement park, right? Well, the Mayor will pose as a little kid who just wandered into the amusement park and wants to take a ride. Then, when they try to get him, we'll fight them."

"But how can the Mayor pretend he's a

kid?" Bubbles asked. "He looks like a Mayor!"

Blossom thought a moment. "We'll have to give him some kid clothes," she said.

"But all we have are dresses," Buttercup pointed out.

"True," Blossom said. "He'll just have to pose as a little girl. Now, which one of you wants to switch clothes with the Mayor?"

"Why does it have to be one of us?" Buttercup said. "Why can't *you* switch with the Mayor?"

"I'm the leader of The Powerpuff Girls!" Blossom said. "I can't be seen fighting bad guys in orange pants, a purple tail-coat, and spats!"

Bubbles pouted. "But I don't like pants," she said, her voice quivering. "I want to keep my pretty blue dress."

"And I'm not switching!" Buttercup announced.

"Oh, Girls, Girls," the Mayor said with a chuckle. "I think you're overlooking the biggest problem with this plan."

"What?" the Girls said together.

The Mayor laughed again. "No matter how you dress me up, no one is ever going to believe that I, the dignified, quick-witted, sharp-minded, sophisticated commander-in-chief of our fair city, am nothing but a silly, bumbling, innocent babe!"

No one said anything for a moment.

"Okay, then, let's go to Plan B," Blossom said.

"Does Plan B include beating these guys to a pulp?" Buttercup asked.

"Of course," Blossom answered.

"Then I'm in!" Buttercup said.

"Does it include giving them another chance to be nice if they want to?" Bubbles asked.

"Not really," Blossom said.

"Does it include snacks?" the Mayor asked.

"Actually . . ." Blossom said, looking around, "it does."

What's this? A plan to catch spooky bad guys that has something to do with snacks? Who ever heard of that?

"Here's what we're going to do," Blossom said. "We'll pretend to leave the amusement park. We'll act like we only came to rescue the Mayor, and now that we've done that we're going. But instead we'll hide."

"*Hide?!*" Buttercup said scornfully. "Powerpuff Girls don't hide! We fight!"

"Powerpuff Girls always use the most effective means of getting the bad guys," Blossom said haughtily. "And if that includes hiding, then that's what we do!"

"Hiding sounds like fun," Bubbles said. "Like playing hide-and-seek with the bad guys!" She giggled. "Where should we hide?"

"In those giant barrels of popcorn over there." Blossom showed them some big wooden vats near a snack stand. "Then we wait for the scary characters to come out. And then we nab 'em!"

The Mayor scratched his chin. "Okay, let me see if I have this straight. We're going to pretend we're leaving with those giant barrels of popcorn over there, but we're really going to hide inside the bad guys —"

"No, Mayor," Blossom said.

The Mayor tried again. "The bad guys are going to pretend to leave, and we're going to hide all that popcorn from them?"

Blossom shook her head in despair.

"Don't worry, Mayor, I'll help you," Bubbles volunteered.

The Girls and the Mayor each climbed into one of the large vats.

After a few moments, the Girls heard footsteps. Carefully, Blossom lifted the lid of her vat just a little. She peered out. In the vat beside her, Buttercup cracked open the lid of her vat. In the next vat, Bubbles did the same. The fourth vat stayed closed. A crunching sound came from inside.

The Girls could see the mummy walking by in front of them. All at once, they leaped out of their vats. Meanwhile, the Mayor stayed behind, snacking.

When the mummy saw The Powerpuff Girls, he started to run. But the Girls were on him in an instant.

The mummy jumped over the kiddie train and raced toward the Mega-Coaster. He leaped into one of the ride's cars.

The Mega-Coaster took off, climbing upward on the track. The Girls zoomed up after it. The Mega-Coaster reached the peak and came barreling down the hill. Then it started up the next hill, the highest one of the ride.

When the cars got to the top of the hill, Buttercup was waiting for them.

"The fun stops here!" she yelled. She grabbed the front car of the Mega-Coaster and braced against it with her super-strength.

"Nice work, Buttercup!" Blossom flew in and whacked the mummy with a punch that sent him flying out of the coaster car.

As the mummy fell toward the ground,

Bubbles grabbed the end of his bandage. The mummy began to unravel. By the time he reached the ground, his bandages were completely off.

Blossom, Buttercup, and Bubbles flew down to the ground. There, standing in front of them, was a tall, slim figure with a green face, slick black hair, and dark sunglasses.

"Ace!" the Girls cried at once.

"Just as I suspected!" Blossom said. "The Gangreen Gang is behind this!"

The Gangreen Gang? Blossom, how did you know?

chapter 7

Buttercup grabbed Ace and flew to the haunted house ride. She threw Ace inside and locked the door.

Meanwhile, Blossom zoomed off after the ghost, who had appeared from behind a game booth. She chased him toward the carousel.

The ghost jumped on the carousel and climbed up on a horse. Blossom flew up to the top of the carousel. She grabbed the point at the top of the ride and began to twirl it like she was spinning a top. The ride spun faster and faster.

Suddenly, the ghost's white sheet came flying off. With it came a brown beret.

There's no mistaking the owner of that brown beret! It belongs to yet another member of the Gangreen Gang!

"Snake!" Blossom yelled accusingly.

Snake flew off the spinning carousel and hit the ground.

"Yessss," Snake said sinisterly.

But Blossom showed no mercy to the sobbing gangster. She picked him up and used her superstrength to hurl him across the park. He smashed right through the window of the haunted house.

Meanwhile, Bubbles had spotted the goblin.

"You may be cute, but that doesn't mean I'm going to go easy on you!" she cried, flying after him.

The goblin began to climb the stairs of the log flume ride. Bubbles zoomed up after him.

At the top of the ride, the goblin stepped into a log. Just as he did, Bubbles grabbed him. The ride started, and they both went flying down the water-filled slide.

Bubbles fought the goblin, punching him and kicking him. Together, they flew up and down the waterways of the log flume, the water splashing them.

The goblin began to cough and sputter.

"What's the matter — did you get some

bubbles up your nose?" Bubbles asked the goblin. "Well, here's some more Bubbles for you!" She socked the goblin as hard as she could in the nose.

The goblin flew out of the ride and landed in the water. A moment later, he surfaced and his goblin mask was gone.

"Little Arturo?" Bubbles said. Who knew the smallest member of the Gangreen Gang could look so cute?

Little Arturo put his hands up to his hair and screamed, "Where's my comb?!"

"Worried about your hair?" Bubbles giggled. "I'll fix it!"

Bubbles grabbed Little Arturo by his hair and swung him around. Then she sent him flying — straight toward the haunted house.

Meanwhile, Buttercup had taken off after the Frankenstein monster, who was headed toward the spinning teacups ride.

The giant Frankenstein monster was trying to stuff himself into one of the cups, but Buttercup grabbed him. She turned her eye beams on him, burning his Frankenstein mask to a crisp.

"Billy!" Buttercup said, recognizing the biggest member of the Gangreen Gang. "I should have known!"

Buttercup flew Billy

over to the haunted house and stuffed him into the chimney.

She turned to her sisters. "Well, only one bad guy left."

"That's right," Blossom said. "The zombie."

That's right, Girls, it's the creepiest, ugliest, scariest-looking amusement park ghoul of them all!

Just then, they spotted the zombie creeping around the side of the fun house.

"Come on! Let's do the triple-split!" Blossom instructed.

The Girls split up, each approaching the zombie from a different direction. Then they all came at him at once.

"Take that!" Blossom cried, socking him in the gut.

"And that!" Buttercup yelled, giving him some lightning-fast kicks.

"And some of that, too!" Bubbles added. She was about to punch him in the nose. But she stopped. "Maybe we should take off his mask first."

"Good idea," Blossom said. She tugged at the corners of the disgusting green mask. But it wouldn't budge.

"Let me try!" Buttercup elbowed her way in front of her sisters. She pulled at the mask, too.

Blossom peered more closely at the zombie's face. Suddenly, those bugged-out eyeballs looked familiar.

"He's not wearing a mask!" she said. "That's Grubber!"

That's right, Girls! This gross Gangreen Gangster doesn't even need a mask to masquerade as a gruesome zombie!

The Girls grabbed Grubber and flew him over to the haunted house. The rest of the Gang was inside, begging to be let out.

"Please! It's scary in here!"

"Help! Let us go!"

"We promise never to do it again!"

Blossom opened the door to the haunted house. "You better not!" she said.

Out came Ace, Snake, Big Billy, and Little Arturo. Grubber joined them.

"I knew it was the Gangreen Gang!" Blossom declared. She pulled the comb she had found earlier out of her pocket. "This is what gave them away!"

"My comb!" Little Arturo wailed.

"See how it feels? Nobody likes to be scared," Bubbles said.

"Why'd you do all this stuff, anyway?" Buttercup demanded.

"We thought if we scared everybody else off we could have the whole park to ourselves," Snake said.

"And our plan would have worked, too, if it weren't for you meddling Girls and the Mayor," grumbled Ace.

"Well, now you'll have a nice jail cell all to yourselves!" Blossom told them. "Right, Mayor? Mayor?"

Mayor! Mayor? Where are you?

Crunch, crunch crunch. The Mayor was still in his vat, munching on popcorn.

The Girls looked at one another and laughed.

Well, it looks like another mystery has been solved. And so, once again, the day is saved, thanks to The Powerpuff Girls!